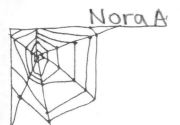

Nora A

CHARLOTTE'S WEB

A Full-Length Play

Adapted from
the book by

E. B. White
l·b white

By

Joseph Robinette

THE DRAMATIC PUBLISHING COMPANY

*** NOTICE ***

CHARLOTTE'S WEB

A Full-Length Play
for Four to Nine Men, Five to Ten Women,
Flexible Ensemble Group*

C H A R A C T E R S

FERN ARABLE . . . . .a young girl
JOHN ARABLE . . . . her father
MARTHA ARABLE . . . . her mother
AVERY ARABLE. . . . . her brother
HOMER ZUCKERMAN . . . . her uncle
EDITH ZUCKERMAN. . . . . her aunt
LURVY. . . . . a hired hand
WILBUR . . . . a pig
TEMPLETON. . . . . .a rat
CHARLOTTE. . . . . a spider
GOOSE, GANDER, SHEEP, LAMB . . . . farm animals
CHORUS
REPORTER, PHOTOGRAPHER, SPECTATORS,
JUDGES, FAIRGOERS, ANNOUNCER,
UNCLE (a pig), SPIDERS . . . . .extras

See Production Notes for flexible casting.

TIME: The Present and The Past
PLACE: The Arables' Farm; the Zuckerman Barn;
the County Fair

the county fair characters

3

WHAT PEOPLE ARE SAYING about *Charlotte's Web*...

"Wonderful writing—fully developed characters and wonderfully comic scenes. Expandable casting is always a great thing because our enrollment is usually high and we need a larger cast. Kids of all ages love this one."   *Carol-Ann Black, Allen Park, Mich.*

"Simple staging was an asset. Very true to original story. The chorus is an ingenious device for bringing in the poetic lyricism of E.B. White. Excellent production notes in script."
Larayne Watts, Willapa Players, Raymond, Wash.

"The children involved loved the play. The children in the audience loved the play. There is a reason the classic tales live on for years—characters that are understandable; a story that speaks to the audience; and a positive message to learn."
Grace Sayers, Theatre Centre, Inc., DeLand, Fla.

"It was well scripted—stayed very close to the book—and was well received by audiences. It sold out every show."
Kara Kemp, Actors Co-Op, Knoxville, Tenn.

"*Charlotte's Web* is a superior adaptation."
Cynthia Zylak, Waterford Elementary School, Waterford, Pa.

"*Charlotte's Web*...has been a delight to produce! It is true to its original novel, with all of the timeless characters and scenes included. It's 'Some Play!' "
Wendi Edwards, Twin Oaks Elementary, Leesburg, Ga.

"Excellent storytelling. Very true to the original text."
Pamela Hendrick, Richard Stockton College of New Jersey, Pomona, N.J.

"One of the best stage adaptations I have ever read. The production charmed audiences, children and adults alike."
Mark Carter, DS Productions, North Vancouver, B.C.

ACT ONE

SCENE: An open space in a farmyard.

AT RISE OF CURTAIN: In darkness, the sounds of a farm *SQ* just before daybreak are heard: crickets, hoot-owls, whip- poorwills, etc. The sounds may be on tape or produced "live" *LQ* offstage by the actors. The lights come up faintly as the CHORUS enters or is revealed onstage.

FIRST MEMBER (to the audience). Shhh! Listen to the sounds of the morning. Very, very early morning. So early, in fact, the sun isn't even up yet.

SECOND MEMBER. Listen to the crickets . . . the hoot-owls . . . a frog down by the pond . . . a dog up at the next farm.

THIRD MEMBER. And today there's another sound. It tells that something exciting happened during the night. Some brand-new pigs were born. (The squealing of young pigs is heard.) *SQ*

FIRST MEMBER. Here's one of them right now — exploring his new home.

5

(WILBUR, a pig, enters in wide-eyed amazement.)

FIRST MEMBER. His name is — well, actually, he doesn't have a name, yet. For the moment, he's still just a little pig. But as you'll see, he isn't just any ordinary pig.

WILBUR. Who am I? Where am I? I've never been here before. (A beat.) I've never been *anywhere* before. Everything seems so strange. But I like it . . . I think.

SECOND MEMBER. The new pig has been born here at the Arables' farm. Before long, you'll meet the Arables. You'll also meet the others — the people *and* the animals — who will play an important part in the little pig's life.

THIRD MEMBER. Now, where should we start? Wait a minute. We've already started. It's early morning. We're at the Arables' farm. Some pigs were born during the night. For now, that's all you need to know. (The CHORUS MEMBERS exit as the lights come up full. A rooster crows. Delighted, WILBUR looks off in the direction of the sound. He excitedly explores his new environment until he hears offstage voices.)

FERN (offstage). Where's Papa going with that ax?

MRS. ARABLE (offstage). Out to the hoghouse. Some pigs were born last night.

FERN (offstage). I don't see why he needs an ax.

MRS. ARABLE (offstage). Well, one of the pigs is a runt. It's very small and weak. (WILBUR looks about in alarm, then points to himself and mouths "me?") So your father has decided to do away with it. (WILBUR runs to a downstage corner in fear.)

FERN (offstage). I've got to stop him.

(FERN, a young girl, enters hurriedly.)

FERN. Papa can't kill it just because it's smaller than the others.

(MARTHA ARABLE, Fern's mother, enters.)

MRS. ARABLE. Stop, Fern! Don't yell. Your father is right. The pig would probably die anyway. (FERN spots WILBUR. She looks at him lovingly for a moment, then starts toward him.)

(JOHN ARABLE, Fern's father, enters from another direction, carrying an ax.)

FERN (shielding WILBUR who cringes behind her). Papa, please don't kill it. It's unfair. (WILBUR nods vigorously.)

ARABLE. Fern, I know more about raising a litter of pigs than you do. A weakling makes trouble. Now run along!

FERN. But it's unfair. The pig couldn't help being born small, could it? (WILBUR shakes his head.) This is the most terrible case of injustice I ever heard of. (WILBUR nods.)

MRS. ARABLE. Fern! (Hopelessly, to ARABLE.) John? (FERN and WILBUR fold their hands pleadingly.)

ARABLE (after a pause). Oh . . . all right. I'll let you take care of it for a little while. (WILBUR collapses in relief.)

FERN (hugging ARABLE). Thank you, Papa. (She runs to WILBUR and pets him.)

MRS. ARABLE. You can start him on a bottle, like a baby. I'll go look for one. (She exits.)

(AVERY, Fern's older brother, enters. He carries an air rifle in one hand and a wooden dagger in the other.)

AVERY. What's going on? What's Fern doing over there?

ARABLE. Your sister has a guest for breakfast, Avery. In fact, for a little while, she's going to be raising that pig.

AVERY (taking a closer look at WILBUR). You call that miserable thing a pig? (WILBUR turns his nose up at the remark.) He's nothing but a runt. (WILBUR tries to draw himself up in a "he-man" pose, but is not very successful. AVERY laughs.)

ARABLE. Come in the house and eat your breakfast, Avery. The school bus will be along in half an hour.

FERN (playing with WILBUR). I'm going to have such a good time with this little pig.

AVERY. Can I have a pig, too, Pop?

ARABLE. No. I only distribute pigs to early risers who are trying to rid the world of injustice. Let's eat. (He and AVERY exit.)

(MRS. ARABLE enters.)

MRS. ARABLE. Fern, honey, I found a baby's nursing bottle and a rubber nipple. I'll pour some warm milk in it. Bring your pig in, and give him some breakfast. Say, what's his name, anyway?

FERN. Why, I don't know.

MRS. ARABLE. Hurry along now. (She exits.)

FERN. My very own pig. (WILBUR smiles.) Now, I have to name you. A perfect name for a perfect pig. (She thinks for a moment.) Fred. That's a good name . . . but not for you.

Clarence . . . no, you don't look like a Clarence . . . Maximil-
ion. Because you're worth a million to me. (A pause. BOTH
laugh and shake their heads.) Maybe I'm trying too hard. Let's
see . . . Barney, Herman, Lawrence, Newton, Morris, Warren,
Willie, Wilbur, William . . . (WILBUR nudges her.) Wait a minute. Wilbur. (WILBUR nods. FERN tries out the name.)
Willll-bur. (WILBUR smiles and nods vigorously.) Wilbur!
What a beautiful name!

MRS. ARABLE (offstage). Breakfast, Fern!

FERN. I'm coming! I mean *we're* coming. Fern and *Wilbur*!
(She takes Wilbur's hand, then they exit.)

(CHORUS MEMBERS enter from various locales.)

FIRST MEMBER. Wilbur.

SECOND MEMBER. Wilbur.

THIRD MEMBER. Wilbur.

FIRST MEMBER. Fern loved Wilbur more than anything.

SECOND MEMBER. Every morning, as soon as she got up, she
warmed his milk, tied his bib on, and warmed his bottle for
him.

(WILBUR enters wearing a bib and sucking a bottle. A moment
later, FERN enters carrying her school books. She pats
WILBUR on the head.)

THIRD MEMBER. After breakfast, Wilbur always walked out to
the road with Fern and waited till her bus came. (FERN and
WILBUR cross to the side of the stage.)

FERN. Now you be a good boy until I get home. (A bus horn SQ
sounds. *This may be done offstage or the sound may be*

made by a CHORUS MEMBER.) There's the bus. 'Bye, 'bye, Wilbur. I'll see you this afternoon. (She hugs WILBUR as the horn sounds again.) Coming! (They wave to each other as she exits. WILBUR slowly crosses to C and resumes sucking his bottle.)

FIRST MEMBER. Every day was a happy day for Wilbur.

SECOND MEMBER. And every night was peaceful.

THIRD MEMBER. He was very contented living with Fern and the Arable family.

WILBUR. I *love* it here.

(MRS. ARABLE enters carrying a bowl.)

MRS. ARABLE. Wilbur, you're getting big enough to have something besides just milk. Try this bowl of cornmeal mush and honey. (She hands the bowl to WILBUR, who eagerly sips from it. MRS. ARABLE removes his bib, takes his bottle, and exits.)

FIRST MEMBER. No longer was Wilbur a runt. (WILBUR pulls himself up.)

SECOND MEMBER. He was growing each day. (Somewhat cockily, WILBUR strikes a pose.)

THIRD MEMBER. He was becoming quite a specimen of a pig.

WILBUR (flexing a muscle). I chalk it up to good, clean living.

ARABLE (offstage). Suppertime, Wilbur.

WILBUR. And to good, fattening food.

(ARABLE enters carrying a bucket.)

ARABLE. Okay, pig, it's time you graduated to slops. Skim

milk, potato skins, leftover sandwiches and marmalade **drippings**. (WILBUR repeats each item after ARABLE with growing enthusiasm. He fairly swoons as ARABLE hands him the bucket, takes the bowl, and exits. WILBUR quickly drinks from the bucket, stopping occasionally to chew.)

FIRST MEMBER. Before long, Wilbur was five weeks old.

WILBUR. I'd say it's about time for a birthday party.

SECOND MEMBER. He was big.

WILBUR. *Now* let them call me a runt.

THIRD MEMBER. And strong.

WILBUR. Anyone for arm-wrestling?

FIRST MEMBER. And healthy.

WILBUR. Check out the pink in the cheeks.

ENTIRE CHORUS. *And* he was ready to be sold.

WILBUR. For a pretty fair price, I'm willing to . . . (A beat, then with panic.) *Sold*! Oh, no! (The CHORUS exits as WILBUR drops his bucket and collapses.)

FERN (offstage). No, Papa, you can't sell him. You just can't.

(ARABLE enters, followed by FERN and MRS. ARABLE.)

ARABLE. He's eating too much. I can't provide for him any longer. I've already sold Wilbur's ten brothers and sisters. (FERN runs to the trembling WILBUR. She sobs and embraces him.)

FERN. Oh, Wilbur. Wilbur!

MRS. ARABLE (after a beat). Listen, everybody. I have a suggestion. Why don't we call the Zuckermans? Your Uncle Homer sometimes raises a pig. And if Wilbur goes there to live, you can walk down the road and visit him anytime you like.

i need homer on stage

FERN. Oh, yes. *Please*, Papa.

ARABLE (after a pause). That's not a bad idea, Martha. Come along. We'll call Uncle Homer. (He picks up the bucket. FERN and WILBUR embrace in great relief, then shake hands.)

FERN. Can Wilbur come, too?

ARABLE. Why not? Maybe we'll let him make the call himself. (He and MRS. ARABLE laugh as they start to exit.)

FERN. It's not funny. He *can* talk, you know.

MRS. ARABLE. Oh, Fern. What an imagination! (ALL exit.)

(The scene shifts to the Zuckerman barn. A moment later HOMER ZUCKERMAN enters with his wife, EDITH, and LURVY, a hired hand. HOMER carries a pig trough and LURVY holds an armload of straw.)

EDITH. Homer Zuckerman, I want to know where you plan to keep that pig.

HOMER (setting the trough down). Right over here in the barn, Edith. Lurvy, go out there and patch up that piece of fence that's coming down.

LURVY (setting the straw down). Sure thing, Mr. Zuckerman. (He exits.)

HOMER. I'll slide this door back so he can't get in there where the cows are. (He slides a sizeable door at R across an opening. A large spider web is revealed behind the door as it is moved.)

EDITH. Well, I just hope this pig's not going to be more trouble than it's worth.

HOMER (completing the moving of the door). Now, I couldn't turn down Fern, could I? She seemed so desperate. (LURVY is heard hammering offstage.) Anyway, she only asked six dollars for it. When the pig gets big enough to slaughter, he'll be worth a lot more than six dollars.

EDITH (cleaning up). Ugh. Dirt, spider webs . . .

HOMER. Perfect for a pig.

FERN (offstage). Uncle Homer! Aunt Edith!

EDITH. Here they are.

(FERN enters with WILBUR.)

FERN. Hi. This is Wilbur.

HOMER (laughing). Oh, he has a name, does he?

(LURVY enters.)

LURVY. All finished, Mr. Zuckerman. (He spots WILBUR.) Well, here's our new boarder.

EDITH. Fern, honey, I just opened a big can of peaches. You come in and have a dish with us.

FERN. Okay, thanks. But let me stay with Wilbur just for a minute . . . till he gets used to his surroundings. (EDITH, HOMER and LURVY exit. For a moment FERN and WIL-BUR look about.) It's very nice here, Wilbur. (WILBUR smiles.) And I can come down and visit you almost every day. (WILBUR nods.) Now I'd better go. I'll see you tomorrow. (They wave to each other as FERN exits.)

WILBUR (after a beat, looking about). It's a very large barn. And old, I'll bet. I like the smell. Hay and manure. Horses and cows. It has a peaceful smell . . . as though nothing bad could happen ever again in the world. (A beat.) Fern was right. It *is* very nice here. (He yawns, lies down, and closes his eyes.)

(A moment later, a GOOSE enters, followed by a GANDER. They circle WILBUR, studying him carefully.)

GOOSE. Hello, hello, hello.

WILBUR (a bit startled). Who . . . who are you?

GOOSE. The Goose.

WILBUR. Oh. Hi, Goose.

GOOSE. And this is my friend, the Gander, Gander, Gander.

WILBUR. But I only see one Gander. You introduced me to three.

GOOSE. No, no, no.

GANDER. We tend to repeat, repeat, repeat ourselves.

GOOSE. Do you have a name . . . besides "pig?"

WILBUR. Yes. They call me Wilbur.

TEMPLETON (offstage). Wilbur? That's a pretty tacky name, if you ask me.

GOOSE. Well, nobody, nobody, nobody asked you.

WILBUR. Who was that?

GANDER. Templeton, the rat.

(TEMPLETON, a rat, enters. He carries string, a tin can, and an orange.)

TEMPLETON. In person. (He stares at WILBUR.) Well, I will admit it's nice to have a pig around the place again. I haven't had delicious, leftover slops in an age.

WILBUR. But the slops will be for me.

TEMPLETON. I'm sure you'll find it in your charitable little heart to share your food with dear old Templeton. Especially if I make a nest right here beside your trough. (He arranges the straw at one side of the trough and buries the string, can, and orange.)

SHEEP (offstage). What's all the commotion in here?

GANDER. It's the old, old Sheep.

GOOSE. And the little, little Lamb.

(The SHEEP and LAMB enter.)

GANDER. We have a new resident.

GOOSE. His name is Wilbur.

LAMB (unenthused). Oh, yeah. The pig.

WILBUR. You know about me?

SHEEP. We overheard the Zuckermans discussing you. They plan to keep you nice and comfortable.

LAMB. And fatten you up with delicious slops.

WILBUR (delighted). Oh, I *am* going to like it here.

SHEEP. Just the same, we don't envy you. You know why they want to make you fat and tender, don't you?

WILBUR. No, I don't.

GOOSE. Now, now, now, old Sheep. He'll learn soon enough.

WILBUR. Learn what?

SHEEP (after a beat). Oh, nothing. Nothing at all. Nice to meet you . . . Wilbur. Lamb, mind your manners.

LAMB (not meaning it). Nice . . . to . . . meet . . . you . . . Wilbur.

WILBUR (a bit concerned). My pleasure, I'm sure.

GOOSE. Well, I have eggs to hatch.

TEMPLETON. And I have trash piles to raid.

GANDER. Good, good, good night, Wilbur. Better get some rest after such a long day.

WILBUR. Yes, thank you, I will. (GOOSE, GANDER, SHEEP, LAMB, and TEMPLETON exit.) The animals seem nice . . . I think. But I'm not sure about Templeton. (A beat.) And I'm a trifle concerned about the old Sheep's remark. (Slightly imitating the Sheep's voice.) "You know why they want to make you fat and tender, don't you?" . . . Well, I don't know. And old Sheep didn't tell me. Well, I'm not going to worry about it just now. I'm much too tired. (He yawns, lies down, and closes his eyes. The lights slowly dim.)

(CHARLOTTE, a spider, comes out from behind the web. She is attached to it by a long drag line. She carefully creeps over to WILBUR and smiles.)

CHARLOTTE (quietly). Go to sleep, Wilbur. Go to sleep, little pig. (She crosses back upstage and disappears behind the web. WILBUR continues to sleep in the dim light.)

(The CHORUS enters. There are noises of thunder, lightning, and rain. *These may be done offstage or by the CHORUS.* The lights come up slowly as WILBUR stirs.)

WILBUR. Oh, no. Morning already. And it's raining. In my dreams, I had made such grand plans for today. Let's see.

FIRST MEMBER. Six-thirty.

WILBUR. Breakfast.

SECOND MEMBER. Seven o'clock.

WILBUR. A nap indoors.

THIRD MEMBER. Eight o'clock.

WILBUR. A nap outdoors. (He is dejected.) *In the sun.*

FIRST MEMBER. Nine o'clock.

WILBUR. Dig a hole.

SECOND MEMBER. Ten o'clock.

WILBUR. Fill up the hole.

THIRD MEMBER. Eleven o'clock.

WILBUR. Just stand still and watch the flies. And the bees and the swallows.

FIRST MEMBER. Twelve noon.

WILBUR. Lunch.

SECOND MEMBER. One o'clock.

WILBUR. Sleep.

THIRD MEMBER. Two o'clock.

WILBUR. Scratch itchy places by rubbing against the fence.

FIRST MEMBER. Three o'clock.

WILBUR. A visit from Fern.

SECOND MEMBER. Four o'clock.

WILBUR. Supper. And four-thirty on . . .

ENTIRE CHORUS. Free time!

WILBUR (moaning). Right. I get everything all beautifully planned out, and it has to go and rain. (There is one final outburst of thunder and lightning, then the CHORUS exits.) SQ LQ I'm lonesome. And I know Fern won't come in such bad weather. Oh, *honestly*. I'm less than two months old, and already I'm tired of living.

(LURVY, in hat and raincoat, enters with a bucket.)

COSTUME↑

LURVY. Morning, pig. Breakfast time. Lots of good leftovers today. (He pours the slops into the trough.) A meal fit for a pig! (WILBUR sniffs it, then turns away.) What's wrong with you? (A beat.) We must have a sick pig here. (He calls offstage.) Mr. Zuckerman! Come out to the barn.

(He exits.)

WILBUR. It does look delicious. But I don't want food. I want love. I want a friend. Someone who will play with me.

CHARLOTTE (offstage). Do you want a friend, Wilbur? I'll be a friend to you. I watched you all night, and I like you.

WILBUR. Where are you? And *who* are you?

HOMER (offstage). I think this will do the trick, Lurvy.

(HOMER, with a container and spoon, and LURVY enter.)

HOMER. Now he won't like this medicine, so you hold him and I'll feed it to him. (LURVY grabs WILBUR who protests.) Come on, boy. This is sulphur and molasses. It'll cure what ails you.

LURVY. Okay, dose him up, Mr. Zuckerman. (HOMER gives WILBUR a spoonful. WILBUR gags.) There, that wasn't so bad, was it? (WILBUR makes a face and nods vigorously.)

HOMER. I think I'll give you a second dose, just for good measure. (He forces another spoonful down WILBUR who gags again.) Good work, Lurvy. That pig will be well in no time. (He and LURVY exit. WILBUR catches his breath and clears his throat.)

WILBUR. Attention, please! Will the party who just spoke to me make himself or herself known? (A pause.) Please tell me where you are if you are my friend.

(CHARLOTTE enters.)

CHARLOTTE. Salutations.

WILBUR (excitedly). Oh, hello. What are salutations?

CHARLOTTE. It's a fancy way of saying "hello."

WILBUR. Oh. And salutations to you, too. Very pleased to meet you. What is your name, please? May I have your name?

CHARLOTTE. My name is Charlotte.

WILBUR. Charlotte what?

CHARLOTTE. Charlotte A. Cavatica. I'm a spider.

WILBUR. I think you're beautiful.

CHARLOTTE. Thank you.

WILBUR. And your web is beautiful, too.

CHARLOTTE. It's my home. I know it looks fragile. But it's really very strong. It protects me. And I trap my food in it.

WILBUR. I'm so happy you'll be my friend. In fact, it restores my appetite. (He begins to eat.) Will you join me?

CHARLOTTE. No, thank you. My breakfast is waiting for me on the other side of my web.

WILBUR. Oh. What are you having?

CHARLOTTE. A fly. I caught it this morning.

WILBUR (choking). You eat . . . flies?

CHARLOTTE. And bugs. Actually, I drink their blood.

WILBUR. Ugh!

CHARLOTTE. That's the way I'm made. I can't help it. Anyway, if I didn't catch insects and eat them, there would soon be so many they'd destroy the earth, wipe out everything.

WILBUR. Really? I wouldn't want *that* to happen.

CHARLOTTE. Now, if you'll excuse me, I'm going to have my breakfast. (She exits behind the web.)

WILBUR (with uncertainty). Well, I've got a new friend, all right. But Charlotte is . . . brutal, I think. And bloodthirsty. How can I learn to like her, even though she is pretty, and very clever, it seems. (He glances back at the web, then slowly lies down.)

(The CHORUS enters.)

Light color changes

FIRST MEMBER. Wilbur was suffering the doubts and fears that often go with finding a new friend.

SECOND MEMBER. But as the days passed by, he slowly discovered that Charlotte had a kind heart and that she was loyal and true.

THIRD MEMBER. Spring soon became summer.

FIRST MEMBER. The early summer days are a jubilee for birds. From the woods, the white-throated sparrow.

SECOND MEMBER. Oh, peabody, peabody, peabody, peabody, peabody, peabody. (WILBUR listens with delight.)

FIRST MEMBER. From the apple trees, the phoebe bird.

THIRD MEMBER. Phoebe, phoe-bee; phoebe, phoe-bee; phoebe, phoe-bee.

FIRST MEMBER. The song sparrows in the birches.

SECOND MEMBER. Sweet, sweet, sweet interlude; sweet, sweet, sweet interlude; sweet, sweet, sweet interlude. (The SECOND and THIRD MEMBERS softly continue the sounds of the birds.)

FIRST MEMBER. The early summer days on a farm are the happiest and fairest of the year. Lilacs and apple blossoms bloom. The days grow warm and soft. And now that school was over, Fern could visit the barn almost every day.

(FERN enters as the ANIMALS, except the GOOSE, enter and greet her with animal sounds which soon give way to clear voices.)

FERN. Hi, everybody! (She sits on the stool. The CHORUS exits and the bird sounds fade.) Wilbur, here's a little piece of pineapple-upside-down cake for you. (WILBUR applauds, takes the cake, and begins to eat.) May I stay and visit for a little while? (WILBUR nods vigorously and the other ANIMALS agree.)

CHARLOTTE (on a perch near her web, looking offstage). Attention, everyone. I have an announcement. After four weeks of unremitting effort on the part of our friend, the Goose, the Goslings have arrived. (ALL act excited as the Goslings chirp offstage.) And here comes the proud mother right now.

(The GOOSE flutters in as ALL applaud.)

GOOSE. Thank you, thank you, thank you. (She bows, then embraces the GANDER.)

CHARLOTTE. And the father is also to be congratulated. (There is lighter applause.)

GANDER. We're pleased as we can be, be, be.

WILBUR (looking offstage). How many Goslings are there?

GOOSE. Seven.

TEMPLETON. I thought there were eight eggs. What happened to the other egg?

GOOSE. It didn't hatch. It was a dud, I guess.

TEMPLETON. Can I have it?

GANDER. Certainly, -ertainly, -ertainly. Add it to your nasty collection. (TEMPLETON exits.)

WILBUR. Imagine wanting a junky old rotten egg.

CHARLOTTE (laughing lightly). A rat is a rat. But, my friends, let's hope that egg never breaks. A rotten egg is a regular stink bomb.

(TEMPLETON enters with the egg.)

TEMPLETON. Don't worry. I won't break it. I handle stuff like this all the time. I'll put it right here under the trough with my other things. (He does so.)

FERN. Oh, Wilbur, I have some good news. Uncle Homer and Aunt Edith seem to be glad that you're putting on weight. (WILBUR beams.)

LAMB. Sure they are.

SHEEP. And you know why, don't you?

WILBUR. You asked me that once before, but you didn't tell me why.

GOOSE. Now, now, now, old Sheep.

SHEEP. He has to know sometime.

WILBUR. Know what?

SHEEP. Wilbur, I don't like to spread bad news. But they're fattening you up because they're going to kill you.

WILBUR (dismayed). They're going to *what*? (FERN is rigid on her stool.)

SHEEP. Kill you. Turn you into smoked bacon and ham. It'll happen when the weather turns cold. It's a regular conspiracy.

WILBUR. Stop! I don't want to die. I want to stay with all my friends. I want to breathe the beautiful air and lie in the beautiful sun.

LAMB. You're certainly making a beautiful noise.

WILBUR. But I don't want to die.

CHARLOTTE. Wilbur, quiet down. (A beat as WILBUR tries to control himself.) You shall not die.

WILBUR. What? Who's going to save me?

CHARLOTTE. I am.

WILBUR. How?

CHARLOTTE. I'm afraid that remains to be seen.

AVERY (offstage). Fern!

FERN. In here, Avery.

(AVERY enters.)

AVERY. Mother sent me to get you. You're going to miss supper.

FERN. Coming. 'Bye, everybody. And thank you, Charlotte, for whatever it is you're going to do to save Wilbur.

AVERY. Who's Charlotte?

FERN. The spider over there.

AVERY. It's tremenjus! (He picks up a stick.)

FERN. Leave it alone.

AVERY. That's a fine spider and I'm going to capture it. (He advances toward CHARLOTTE.)

FERN. You stop it, Avery.

AVERY. I want that spider. (FERN grabs the stick and they fight over it.) Let go of my stick, Fern!

FERN. Stop it! Stop it, I say! (WILBUR waves to FERN that he has an idea. He rushes behind AVERY and kneels, then makes a "pushing" motion with his hands. FERN pushes AVERY over WILBUR. AVERY falls into the trough. The ANIMALS react.)

AVERY. Help!

FERN. I warned you, Avery.

AVERY. That's not fair. You and Wilbur ganged up on me.

FERN (wrinkling her nose). What's that smell?

AVERY. I think we broke a rotten egg. Good night, what a stink! Let's get out of here. (He and FERN exit hurriedly. The SHEEP, LAMB, GOOSE and GANDER flee in different directions, protesting violently.)

TEMPLETON. My beloved egg! (He gathers up the egg and the rest of his belongings and exits.)

CHARLOTTE. I'm glad that's over. I'm sure the smell will go away soon. (A pause.)

WILBUR. Charlotte?

CHARLOTTE. Yes.

WILBUR. Were you serious when you promised you would keep them from killing me?

CHARLOTTE. I've never been more serious in my life.

WILBUR. How are you going to save me?

CHARLOTTE. Well, I really don't know. But I want you to get plenty of sleep and stop worrying. (WILBUR stretches out on the straw as the lights begin to dim.)

WILBUR. Okay. Good night, Charlotte.

CHARLOTTE. Good night, Wilbur. (A pause.)

WILBUR. Thank you, Charlotte.

CHARLOTTE. Good night. (The barn is now in shadows. WILBUR falls asleep.) What to do. What to do. I promised to save his life, and I am determined to keep that promise. But how? (A pause.) Wait a minute. The way to save Wilbur is to play a trick on Zuckerman. If I can fool a bug, I can surely fool a man. People are not as smart as bugs. (A beat.) Of course. That's it. This will not be easy, but it must be done. (She turns her back on the audience.) First, I tear a section out of the web and leave an open space in the middle. Now, I shall weave new threads to take the place of the ones I removed. (She chants slightly.) Swing spinnerets. Let out the thread. The longer it gets, the better it's read. (She begins to "write" with elaborate movements, though her actions are deliberately indistinguishable.) Atta girl. Attach. Pay out line. Descend. Complete the curve. Easy now. That's it. Back up.

Take your time. Now tie it off. Good. (She chants.) The message is spun. I've come to the end. The job that I've done is all for my friend. (She steps aside as a special light reveals the words "Some Pig" written in the web. *The center part of the web may be affixed with velcro to the rest of the web. It can then be pulled off and discreetly discarded by Charlotte. Underneath would be the now-exposed writing which should be similarly velcroed over the next writing and so on.* She reads aloud.) Some pig. (She smiles.) Not bad, old girl, for the first time around. But it *was* quite exhausting. I'd better catch a little nap before daybreak. (She exits behind the web. The lights begin to brighten and a rooster crows. WILBUR stirs. He is having a bad dream.)

WILBUR. No, no. Please don't. Stop! (He wakes up.) Oh, my goodness. That was a terrible dream. There were men with guns and knives coming out here to take me away.

(LURVY enters with a bucket. WILBUR retreats slightly.)

LURVY. Here you go, pig. Breakfast. Leftover pancakes, half a doughnut, stale toast. (He sets the bucket down.) Absolutely de . . . de . . . (He sees the writing in the web.) What's that? I'm seeing things. (He calls offstage.) Mr. Zuckerman! Mr. Zuckerman! I think you'd better come out to the pig pen quick! (He exits hurriedly.)

WILBUR (unaware of the writing in the web). What did he see? There's nothing here but me. (He feels himself.) That's it! He saw me! He saw that I'm big and healthy and . . . and ready to be made into . . . ham. They're coming out here right now with guns and knives. I just know it. What can I do? (A beat.)

Wait! The fence that Lurvy patched up. Maybe it's loose again.
I have to get out. I have no choice. It's either freedom . . . or
the frying pan. (He spots the bucket.) But, first, a little
sustenance. (He drinks from the bucket.) Now, I'm ready.
I'm breaking out of this prison. They'll never take me alive!
(A beat.) What am I saying? I've got to get out of here. (He
starts to rush offstage.) Chaaarrrge! (He runs off. A crash is
heard offstage.)

(CHARLOTTE enters, yawning.)

CHARLOTTE. What was that? Wilbur, where are you?
WILBUR (from offstage). I'm free!
HOMER (from offstage). Now, Lurvy, what could be so im-
  portant that you had to drag me out here before I've finished —
LURVY (from offstage). You'll see, Mr. Zuckerman. You'll see.

(HOMER and LURVY enter.)

HOMER. All I can see is . . . the pig's not here!
LURVY. What?
HOMER. Look out there in the chicken yard. (He points off-
  stage.) He's escaped. Edith's out there gathering eggs. Maybe
  she can head him off. Let's go!
LURVY. But . . . look at the spider web, Mr. Zuckerman.
HOMER. No time right now. Gotta catch that pig. (He and
  LURVY exit. From offstage.) Edith! The pig's out! Run him
  back this way! Pig's out!
CHARLOTTE. Oh, no.

(SHEEP and LAMB enter.)

SHEEP. What's all the fuss?
LAMB. This racket is killing my ears.

(GOOSE and GANDER enter.)

GOOSE. There's so much noise, noise, noise.
GANDER. The Goslings can't sleep. (Offstage noises are heard.)

(WILBUR enters, chased by EDITH, HOMER and LURVY. The
    ANIMALS cheer WILBUR.)

ANIMALS. Go, Wilbur, go! Don't let them catch you! Run,
    run, run! (WILBUR does a U-turn and exits, eluding the
    OTHERS. They exit behind WILBUR. The chase is heard off-
    stage.)
CHARLOTTE. Now stop this! Don't encourage him. If Wilbur
    does escape, he'll never stand a chance in the outside world.
    So, if he runs through here again, we've got to stop him. (The
    chase is heard coming closer.) Get set! Here he comes.

(WILBUR runs in.)

WILBUR. I'll make it this time! I saw an open gate that leads to
    the woods. Thank you, everybody, for all your — (The ANI-
    MALS tackle him and hold him down.) What is this? Even my
    friends have turned against me! (The OTHERS are heard off-
    stage. WILBUR squirms as he is held down.) I'll not go down
    without a fight! I'll struggle all the way to the butcher block!

I won't be bacon for anybody!

(HOMER, LURVY and EDITH enter breathlessly. The ANI-
MALS quickly let go of WILBUR whose bravado disappears
quickly as he cowers.)

HOMER. Well, you certainly gave us a run for our —
LURVY. Mr. Zuckerman. Mrs. Zuckerman. Look! This is what
I wanted to show you. (He points to the web. ALL stare at it
for a moment. WILBUR and the ANIMALS look, too.)
HOMER (amazed). A miracle has happened on this farm.
LURVY. A miracle.
EDITH. I don't believe it! "Some Pig." (WILBUR begins to re-
gain his confidence.)
HOMER. It is clear we have no ordinary pig.
EDITH. It seems to me we have no ordinary *spider*.
HOMER. Oh, no, it's the pig that's unusual. Edith, call the min-
ister and tell him about the miracle. Then call the Arables.
Hurry. (EDITH exits as WILBUR rises and sits happily on a
barrel or box near the web.) You know, Lurvy, I've thought all
along that pig of ours was an extra good one.
LURVY. He's quite a pig.
HOMER. I'd say he's . . . "some pig." (He and LURVY laugh.)
Well, let's hurry and get the chores done. I'm sure we'll have
lots of visitors when word of this leaks out. (He and LURVY
exit. The ANIMALS cheer, applaud, and congratulate CHAR-
LOTTE.)
WILBUR (himself again). Oh, Charlotte. Thank you. Thank
you. Thank you.

CHARLOTTE.   It seems to have worked.   At least for the present.   But if we are to save Wilbur's life, I will have to write more words in the web.   And I need new ideas.   Any suggestions?

LAMB. How about "Pig Supreme?"

CHARLOTTE. No good. It sounds like a rich dessert.

GOOSE. How about "terrific, terrific, terrific?"

CHARLOTTE. Cut that down to one "terrific" and it will do very nicely. I think it might impress Zuckerman. Does anybody here know how to spell "terrific?"

GANDER.   I think it's tee, double ee, double rr, double rr, double eye, double ff, double eye, double see, see, see, see, see.

CHARLOTTE. What kind of acrobat do you think I am?

GANDER. Sorry. Sorry. Sorry.

CHARLOTTE. I'll spell the word the best way I can.

SHEEP (glancing offstage R).   Look, here comes Templeton. Maybe he can help with this project.

(TEMPLETON enters R.)

TEMPLETON. Templeton only helps himself. What's up?

SHEEP. Did you see the message in the web?

TEMPLETON. It was there when I went out this morning. It's no big deal.

SHEEP. It was a big deal to Zuckerman. And now Charlotte needs new ideas. When you go to the dump, bring back a clipping from a magazine. Charlotte can copy the words. It will help save Wilbur's life.

TEMPLETON. Let him die. I should worry.

SHEEP. You'll worry next winter when Wilbur is dead and nobody comes down here with a nice pail of slops.

TEMPLETON (after a pause). I'll bring back a magazine clipping.

CHARLOTTE. Thanks. The meeting is adjourned. (The ANIMALS begin to exit, bidding each other farewell as they go.) Tonight, I will tear my web apart and write "terrific." Now go out into the yard and lie in the sun, Wilbur. I need a little rest. I was up all night.

WILBUR (as he exits). Thank you, Charlotte. You're the best friend a pig ever had. (He exits.)

CHARLOTTE (smiling to herself). Some pig. *Some pig.* (The lights fade.) LQ

(The CHORUS enters.) LQ

FIRST MEMBER. As the day went on, the news about the words in Charlotte's web began to spread throughout the county.

SECOND MEMBER. People came from miles around to see the words on Charlotte's web.

THIRD MEMBER. News of the wonderful pig spread clear up into the hills where the farmers talked about the miraculous animal on Zuckerman's farm.

FIRST MEMBER. Charlotte knew there would be even more visitors the next day.

SECOND MEMBER. So that night, while the other creatures slept, she began to work on her web.

CHARLOTTE. Swing spinnerets. Let out the thread. The longer it gets, the better it's read. (She begins to "write.")

THIRD MEMBER. Spinning and weaving, she began to form the new letters.

FIRST MEMBER. Again, she talked to herself as though to cheer herself on.

CHARLOTTE. Descend. Pay out line. Whoa, girl. Steady. Now for the R.

SECOND MEMBER. On through the night the spider worked at her difficult task. It was nearly morning when she finally finished.

CHARLOTTE. The message is spun. I've come to the end. The job that I've done is all for my friend.

THIRD MEMBER. She then ate a small bug she was saving. And, after that . . .

CHORUS (softly). She fell asleep. (They exit. A light comes up on the web to reveal the word "Terrific.")

(A moment later, WILBUR enters yawning.)

WILBUR. I can't believe I spent the entire day *and* night outside sleeping. Oh, well. It's very refreshing. Especially in the summer.

(LURVY enters with a bucket.)

LURVY. I'm afraid to look. I know it can't happen again. (He looks over at the web.) I don't believe my eyes. "Terrific." It did! It did happen again! "Terrific." Another miracle! Mr. Zuckerman! Come quick! It's another miracle! (He exits.)

WILBUR (looking at the web). It's beautiful.

(FERN enters.)

FERN. Good morning, Wilbur. (WILBUR motions toward the web.) "Terrific." Hooray for Charlotte! She did it again! (WILBUR shushes her.) Oh, she's still sleeping. It must have been a long night for her. (WILBUR nods.)

HOMER (offstage). Edith, phone the reporter on the *Weekly Chronicle* and tell him what happened!

(HOMER enters, followed by LURVY.)

HOMER. He may want to bring a photographer. (He looks at the web.) Well, what do you know. There it is as plain as day. "Terrific." What do you know!

(ARABLE, MRS. ARABLE and AVERY enter.)

MRS. ARABLE. Did it happen again?

LURVY (pointing to the web). Another miracle!

ARABLE. Homer, you're going to have visitors all over the place today.

HOMER. I don't know where we'll put them. Yesterday, the driveway was practically full of cars and trucks.

ARABLE. We can park the vehicles in the open field. Avery and I will direct traffic.

AVERY. Hooray. I'll be the captain of the Zuckerman police force. (ALL laugh as ARABLE and AVERY exit.)

FERN. Does this mean you're not going to kill Wilbur, Uncle Homer?

HOMER. Who said anything about killing him?

FERN. But that's what happens to pigs. In the cold weather. You know . . . the conspiracy.

MRS. ARABLE. Conspiracy? Where did you get a word like that?

FERN. The old sheep . . . I mean, I guess I picked it up somewhere.

HOMER. Wilbur's safe for now, Fern. As long as he's attracting all this attention. Come on Lurvy. Work to do.

LURVY. Terrific pig. (He and HOMER exit.)

MRS. ARABLE. Fern, your Aunt Edith is doing lots of baking for the visitors today. Let's go help her.

FERN. Can't I stay?

MRS. ARABLE. I think you spend too much time with these animals. You should play with children your own age. Like Tommy Watson.

FERN. Oh, Mother.

MRS. ARABLE. Or Freddy Johnson.

FERN. Yuk.

MRS. ARABLE. Or Henry Fussy.

FERN. Henry Fussy? (She emits a Bronx cheer.)

MRS. ARABLE. Let's go.

FERN. Oh, all right. 'Bye, Wilbur. 'Bye, Charlotte. (She and MRS. ARABLE exit.)

(CHARLOTTE enters, stretching and yawning.)

CHARLOTTE. Good morning, Wilbur.

WILBUR. Oh, Charlotte. Everybody's so excited about the new word. And they're expecting more visitors today. (CHARLOTTE smiles.)

(The GOOSE and GANDER enter.)

GOOSE and GANDER. Morning, morning, morning.

WILBUR. Did you see Charlotte's new word?

GOOSE. Of course, of course, of course. "Terrific" was my idea. Remember?

(The LAMB enters, followed by the SHEEP.)

LAMB. Wilbur, is all this attention going to go to your head and make you stuck up?

WILBUR. Of course not. Fame will never spoil me.

SHEEP. Anyway, he still has to worry about the future. His life is not secure yet.

WILBUR. I know. But I can face anything with friends like you. Friendship is one of the most satisfying things in the world.

(TEMPLETON enters holding the lid of a soapflakes box.)

templeton the rat

TEMPLETON. You'd better believe it, buster. And you'd better not forget the friendship of old Templeton who just happened to be at the dump all night looking for words to save you. (He hands the box lid to CHARLOTTE.) Try this one. It's from an empty package of soapflakes.

CHARLOTTE (reading). "With new, radiant action." (The OTHERS repeat the words approvingly.) Wilbur, run around. I want to see you in action to see if you are radiant. (WILBUR runs about.) Now back again. Faster. (WILBUR obeys.) Jump into the air. (WILBUR jumps as the OTHERS applaud and cheer with increasing intensity as he completes each task.) Do a front flip . . . a back flip . . . and roll over into a split! (In the split, WILBUR smiles and poses.) It may not be radiant, but it's interesting.

WILBUR. Actually, I feel radiant. I really do.

CHARLOTTE. Then radiant you shall be. (ALL cheer. TEMPLETON looks offstage, quiets them, then hides.)

(LURVY enters with the bucket.)

LURVY. Sorry, pig, but I got so excited, I forgot to leave your slops this morning. (He pours the food into the trough as WILBUR begins to eat.) Mrs. Zuckerman even threw in a whole fresh piece of apple strudel she's baking for the visitors. That's what you get for being a terrific pig. Oh, yes. And Mr. Zuckerman's even talking about taking you to the County Fair if all this excitement continues. (He exits. TEMPLETON comes out of hiding.)

WILBUR. Did you hear that, everybody? The County Fair. That means I would get to live for at least another month.

GOOSE. And maybe, maybe, maybe longer.

GANDER. If you win a blue, blue, blue ribbon.

WILBUR. You'll go to the Fair with me, won't you, Charlotte?

CHARLOTTE. I don't know. The Fair comes at a bad time for me. That's when I'll be making my egg sac and filling it with eggs.

WILBUR. You could lay your eggs at the Fair.

LAMB. Nobody's going to the Fair yet. Lurvy said they were just *thinking* about taking you *if* the excitement continues.

CHARLOTTE. Well, that means more new words. So I'd better start another one right away. Now, everybody stand in front of me so the others won't notice that I'm writing if they come back before I finish. (ALL make a line in front of her, standing on boxes, bales of hay, etc. She is now partially hidden.)

Swing spinnerets. Let out the thread. The longer it gets, the better it's read. (She begins to write.)

GOOSE. Templeton would need to go to the Fair, too. Somebody, somebody, somebody has to run errands and do general work.

TEMPLETON. I'm staying right here. I haven't the slightest interest in Fairs.

SHEEP. That's because you've never been to one. A Fair is a rat's paradise. Everybody spills food at a Fair. Popcorn, frozen custard, candy apples.

TEMPLETON. Stop! That's enough! You've twisted my whiskers. I'll go. (ALL applaud.)

CHARLOTTE. Attach, ascend, repeat.

GOOSE (glancing behind herself at CHARLOTTE). Charlotte's working fast, fast, fast.

CHARLOTTE. I've pretty well got the hang of it now.

LAMB (looking off R). Look, here come some visitors.

SHEEP (looking off R). It looks like a reporter and a photographer.

GANDER. Hurry, hurry, hurry, Charlotte.

CHARLOTTE. I'm almost finished. Just have to cross the final "T." Over to the right, pay out line, attach.

LAMB. They're almost here. (ALL are very nervous.)

CHARLOTTE. Repeat, attach . . . and finished. (ALL quickly disassemble their "coverage" of CHARLOTTE and assume natural positions. TEMPLETON partially hides himself. In the web is the word "Radiant.")

HOMER (offstage). Right this way, everybody. Here we are.

(HOMER enters. He is followed by a REPORTER, a PHOTO-GRAPHER, the ARABLES, LURVY, FERN, EDITH and a

CROWD.)

HOMER. Make room for the photographer and the reporter from the *Weekly Chronicle.*

FERN. May I have my picture taken with Wilbur?

REPORTER. Sure, young lady. (FERN poses with WILBUR.)

PHOTOGRAPHER. Say "cheese." (TEMPLETON emerges from his hiding spot, unseen by the PEOPLE.)

TEMPLETON (licking his lips). Cheese? (The LAMB and SHEEP shove him back into hiding.)

FERN. Cheese. (The PHOTOGRAPHER snaps the picture.)

REPORTER. Now you, Mr. Zuckerman.

HOMER. Let me get my wife and my hired hand in here, too. Edith . . . Lurvy. (EDITH and LURVY join HOMER and WILBUR. The PHOTOGRAPHER takes their picture. ALL applaud.)

MRS. ARABLE. Look how big Wilbur's gotten.

ARABLE. You'll get some extra good ham and bacon, Homer, when it comes time to kill *that* pig. (WILBUR sways back and forth, then faints.)

FERN. Somebody help him!

AVERY. I'll be the pig! Hey, watch me! (He kneels next to WILBUR and tosses straw into the air.) Oink, oink, oink! (ALL except FERN and MRS. ARABLE laugh.)

FERN. Oh, keep quiet. Keep *qui*-ut!

MRS. ARABLE. Avery, what do you think you are?

AVERY. A pig! I'm a pig. Oink, oink, oink. (MRS. ARABLE pulls him away from WILBUR.)

FERN (patting Wilbur's cheeks). Wake up, Wilbur! Wake up! (WILBUR comes to and slowly rises as ALL cheer.)

HOMER. Well, that pig *is* terrific, just like it says in the web.

REPORTER. But Mr. Zuckerman, that's not what it says in the web.

HOMER (looking at the web). Glory be!

EDITH. We were so busy chattering, we didn't even notice there's yet another word in the web.

FERN. Radiant.

LURVY. Radiant.

EDITH. Radiant.

HOMER. Well, sir. That does it. I have an announcement that you can print in the newspaper. I'm going to enter this pig in the County Fair. (ALL cheer.) If he can win a blue ribbon, I guarantee we'll never make bacon and ham out of him. (More applause.)

EDITH. Come on, everybody. Let's go to the kitchen and celebrate with some fresh apple strudel and iced tea.

ARABLE. Sounds good, Edith. (The PEOPLE exit. The ANIMALS cheer.)

WILBUR. Charlotte, you did it. Thank you. Thank you.

CHARLOTTE. Well, we got you *to* the Fair. But that's only half the battle.

WILBUR. Will you come with me, Charlotte? *Please.*

CHARLOTTE. I'm not sure. I'm just not sure. (A beat.) Now may I ask everyone to kindly leave? This day has been particularly exhausting, and I must have some rest.

SHEEP. Of course, Charlotte. Come on, Lamb.

TEMPLETON. I'll admit she's earned a little peace and quiet.

GOOSE. Me, me, me, too.

GANDER. Ditto, ditto, ditto.

WILBUR. I'll be out in the sun taking a nap, Charlotte. (ALL, except CHARLOTTE, exit.)

CHARLOTTE. I'm suddenly very tired. I know I won't be able to help Wilbur much longer. I'll have to lay my eggs soon, and I do want them to hatch right here in the barn where it's warm and safe. (A beat.) But I'll take the chance. I *will* go to the Fair with Wilbur. People will be expecting to see a word in the web. It may help him win that blue ribbon, and his whole future — if he's to have a future at all — totally depends on what happens at the Fair. (She goes behind the web and, for a moment, the stage if empty. *An optional intermission may be used at this point.)* LQ SQ

ACT TWO

SCENE: The stage is empty. After a moment, the CHORUS
enters. As they speak, they rearrange the "furnishings" from
the barn to suggest an area in the livestock locale at the Fair,
specifically Wilbur's pen and ample passage room around it.
The UR web is removed and another hung UL.

FIRST MEMBER. The days of summer drifted on.
SECOND MEMBER. Before long, summer was almost gone.
THIRD MEMBER. The end of summer brings many things. Late
harvesting. Thoughts of school. *And* the County Fair. (Carni-
val music is heard.)
FIRST MEMBER. Step right up, ladies and gentlemen. Ride
the giant Ferris wheel. Only ten cents. One thin dime. You
can see the whole county from the top of the giant Ferris
wheel.
SECOND MEMBER. Right over here, fellows. Win a genuine
Navaho blanket. Knock down three cloth cats with three
regulation baseballs, and you're a winner every time.

THIRD MEMBER. Come one, come all! Foot-long hot dogs, giant hamburgers, french fried potatoes. It's all here, and more, at the Lion's Club Barbecue Pavillion.

CHORUS. At the Fair. At the Fair. At the Fair. (They begin to leave.)

FIRST MEMBER. Harness racing.

SECOND MEMBER. Livestock judging.

THIRD MEMBER. Four-H exhibits.

CHORUS. At the Fair. At the Fair. At the Fair. (They exit.)

(HOMER enters. He is followed by WILBUR who is tied to a rope held by FERN.)

HOMER (yelling offstage). We're back! (FERN unties WILBUR and he rolls in the straw.)

(LURVY enters with a pitchfork filled with more straw.)

LURVY. They're mighty generous with their straw around here, Mr. Zuckerman. Thought I'd get a little more to make Wilbur comfortable. (He dumps the straw, then exits.)

(ARABLE enters with a trough. AVERY follows him with a bucket.)

HOMER. Right over here, John. (ARABLE sets the trough down. AVERY pours in the slops.)

AVERY. Pop, can I eat some of Wilbur's slops someday? (WILBUR eats.)

ARABLE. In a way, you already do. What he eats is leftovers from what we eat.

AVERY. Yeah, but it looks better in the bucket than it does on the table.

(MRS. ARABLE enters, holding a washcloth.)

MRS. ARABLE. Well, thank you very much. (She scrubs Avery's face while he squirms.) Hold still, Avery. There's something behind your ears.

(EDITH enters with a sponge and a large jar of buttermilk.)

VOICE ON LOUDSPEAKER (offstage). Attention, please! Will the owner of a Pontiac car, license number H-two, four, three, nine, please move your car away from the fireworks shed!

HOMER (to EDITH, who has begun to bathe WILBUR). What are you doing, Edith?

EDITH. Giving the pig a buttermilk sponge bath. He worked up a sweat when you and Fern took him for that walk just now.

FERN. Can I have some money?

AVERY. Can I, too?

FERN. I'm going to win a doll.

AVERY. I'm going to crash a jet plane into another one. (He demonstrates and almost upsets EDITH.)

MRS. ARABLE. Avery!

AVERY. Sorry, Aunt Edith.

EDITH. It's okay. They're just excited.

FERN. Can I have a balloon?

AVERY. Can I have a cheeseburger?

MRS. ARABLE. You'll have to wait until we can go with you.

ARABLE. Oh, now, Martha. Let's let the children go off by

themselves. The Fair only comes once a year. (FERN and AVERY cheer.)

ARABLE (giving change to FERN and AVERY). Now run along. But don't be gone long.

FERN. Okay, 'bye. Scrub Wilbur up real good, Aunt Edith. He's got to win that blue ribbon tomorrow.

AVERY. Come on, Fern.

ARABLE. Now hurry back. We'll be leaving in a little while. *Tomorrow's* the big day.

FERN. Okay, Papa. (FERN and AVERY exit as the OTHERS call after them.)

ARABLE. Don't eat lots of stuff that's going to make you sick to your stomachs.

MRS. ARABLE. And if you go on those swings, you hang on tight. Hear me?

EDITH. And don't get lost!

MRS. ARABLE. Don't get dirty!

HOMER. Don't get overheated!

ARABLE. Watch out for pickpockets!

EDITH. And don't cross the racetrack when the horses are coming! (A beat.)

MRS. ARABLE. Do you think it's all right, John?

ARABLE. Well, they've got to grow up sometime. And a Fair is a good place to start, I guess. (MRS. ARABLE sighs and blows her nose into the washrag.)

(LURVY enters with a wooden sign reading: "Zuckerman's Famous Pig.")

LURVY. Here's the sign from Wilbur's crate, Mr. Zuckerman.

HOMER. Good, Lurvy. We'll set it right here so everybody will know this is the pig they've been hearing about. (He and LURVY prop the sign up next to Wilbur's pen.) "Zuckerman's Famous Pig."

LURVY. If we're finished for the time being, Mr. Zuckerman, I think I'll go down to the midway and meet some of my friends.

HOMER. Sure thing, Lurvy.

LURVY. Maybe I'll even win one of those Navaho blankets I've been hearing about. (He exits.)

HOMER. It's great to be at the Fair, isn't it? I'm nearly as excited as the kids. Let's go look at the new tractors, Edith.

EDITH (drying WILBUR, who is asleep, with a towel). Let me just dry him off. Look, he's asleep.

ARABLE. Martha, let's you and me wander over to the cattle-barn and see the Holsteins and the Guernseys.

MRS. ARABLE. Okay. But let's try to keep an occasional eye out for Fern and Avery.

EDITH. All finished. (She sets the towel down.)

HOMER. Let's go then.

ARABLE. We'll meet you back here in a little while. (The two COUPLES exit in opposite directions.)

(TEMPLETON appears from behind a crate or box. CHARLOTTE enters from behind the web.)

TEMPLETON. I thought they'd never leave. It's easier for a rat to hide in a barn than out in the open like this. Well, I think I'll do a little exploring.

CHARLOTTE. Please bring me back a word, Templeton.

TEMPLETON. I'll do what I can. (He exits.)

CHARLOTTE. If I don't write something, I'm sure Wilbur will have a difficult time winning that blue ribbon. (She looks at the sleeping WILBUR.) He's a cute little pig, and smart. But I'm sure there will be bigger pigs here. And even better-looking ones.

(UNCLE, a large pig, enters sniffing around. A moment later, he sees CHARLOTTE.)

UNCLE. Hi, there.

CHARLOTTE. May I have your name?

UNCLE. No name. Just call me Uncle.

CHARLOTTE. Very well . . . Uncle. You're rather large. Are you a spring pig?

UNCLE. Sure, I'm a spring pig. What did you think I was, a spring chicken? Haw, haw, that was a good one. Eh, sister?

CHARLOTTE. Mildly funny. I've heard funnier ones, though. What are you doing over here?

UNCLE. They're still working on my pen. I just walked away. They'll come after me when they see I'm gone. But I thought I'd wander around and look at the competition. (He looks down at WILBUR.) Well, no problem here. From what I've seen so far, I've got that blue ribbon all sewed up. But I won't *needle* you about it. Get it? Haw, haw.

VOICE (offstage). Uncle! Where are you, Uncle?

UNCLE. Well, better be getting back. I've got to get spiffy for the crowds that will be coming to admire me. So long, sister. (As he exits, WILBUR wakes up.)

WILBUR (drowsily). Oh, hi, Charlotte. Where is everybody?

CHARLOTTE. Off to see the Fair.

WILBUR. Did I hear you talking to someone?

CHARLOTTE. A pig that's staying next door.

WILBUR. Is he better than me? I mean . . . bigger?

CHARLOTTE. I'm afraid he is much bigger.

WILBUR. Oh, no.

CHARLOTTE. But he has a most unattractive personality. Oh, he's going to be a hard pig to beat on account of his size and weight. But with me helping you, it can be done.

WILBUR. When will you be writing the new word?

CHARLOTTE. Later on, if I'm not too tired. Just spinning this new web earlier today took a lot of my strength.

(Two SPECTATORS enter. CHARLOTTE eases into the background.)

FIRST SPECTATOR. Well, here's a good-looking fellow. (He reads the sign.) "Zuckerman's Famous Pig." (WILBUR smiles.)

SECOND SPECTATOR. Look at his silky white coat. And his nice, curly tail.

FIRST SPECTATOR. I think he's the finest pig we've seen today.

SECOND SPECTATOR (looking offstage). Let's go look at that pig over there. (He exits.)

FIRST SPECTATOR (to WILBUR). I think I've heard of you. Aren't you that "radiant" pig who's supposed to be "terrific?" (WILBUR smiles and nods.)

SECOND SPECTATOR (offstage). Look over here at *this* pig. (The FIRST SPECTATOR exits.) He's gigantic.

FIRST SPECTATOR (offstage). And he seems to be *very* confident.

SECOND SPECTATOR (offstage). He may get the blue ribbon after all.

FIRST SPECTATOR (offstage). Well, let's go look at the horses and see if we can pick the winner over there.

WILBUR. Oh, dear. Did you hear that, Charlotte?

CHARLOTTE. Chin up, young friend. Those weren't the judges. They were merely the spectators. The judges are the ones who count.

(TEMPLETON enters carrying an article torn from a newspaper.)

TEMPLETON (handing it to CHARLOTTE). Well, here's your order.

CHARLOTTE. I hope you brought a good one. It is the last word I shall ever write.

WILBUR (alarmed). Charlotte, what do you mean?

CHARLOTTE (studying the article). Templeton, my eyes seem to be going. I'm having trouble reading this. What's the word?

TEMPLETON. "Humble." (He spells it out.) H-u-m-b-l-e.

CHARLOTTE. Humble has two meanings. It means "not proud" and it means "close to the ground." That's Wilbur all over.

TEMPLETON. Well, I hope you're satisfied. I'm not going to spend all my time delivering papers. I came to this Fair to enjoy myself.

CHARLOTTE. You've been very helpful, Templeton. You may run along now.

TEMPLETON. I'm going to make a night of it. The old sheep was right. This Fair is a rat's paradise. What eating! What drinking! 'Bye, 'bye, my humble Wilbur. Fare thee well, Charlotte, you old schemer! This will be a night to remember in a rat's life. (He exits.)

WILBUR. Charlotte, what did you mean when you said this would be your last word?

CHARLOTTE. Shhh!
WILBUR. But, Charlotte . . .

(HOMER enters with his arm around LURVY who holds a blanket. EDITH follows them in.)

HOMER. That's terrific! Good for you, Lurvy.
LURVY. Just lucky, that's all.

(HOMER motions to ARABLE, MRS. ARABLE and AVERY, who is eating a candy apple and has a balloon tied to his ear, as they enter from the other side of the stage.)

HOMER. Hey, everybody. Look what Lurvy won.
AVERY. What is it, Lurvy?
LURVY. A genuine Navaho blanket.
ARABLE (inspecting the blanket). Well, congratulations.
MRS. ARABLE (looking about). I do wonder where Fern is.
ARABLE. She'll be along.
HOMER. Well, I suppose we ought to think about getting home.
AVERY. Will the pig be okay?
HOMER. Sure, Avery. They have night watchmen to look after the animals after the people leave.
EDITH (petting WILBUR). He'll be fine.
HOMER. Get lots of sleep, Wilbur. The judges come around first thing in the morning.
ARABLE. They may even get here before we do.

(FERN enters with a doll and carrying Crackerjacks.)

FERN. Look at the doll I won, everybody.

AVERY. Well, it's a lucky day today.

HOMER. Let's just hope it's as lucky for Wilbur tomorrow.

MRS. ARABLE. Fern, I've been worried. Where were you?

FERN. I met Henry Fussy, and he invited me to ride with him on the Ferris wheel.

MRS. ARABLE (brightening). Henry Fussy?

FERN. He even bought a ticket for me.

MRS. ARABLE. My, my.

HOMER. Let's load up, everybody. (ALL begin to exit. FERN and MRS. ARABLE are the last to go.)

FERN. I hope you weren't *too* worried about me.

MRS. ARABLE. Not really. Now that I know where you were.

FERN. I'll be thinking about you tonight, Wilbur. (She crosses to WILBUR.) Good luck, tomorrow. Sleep well. (She pats WILBUR. WILBUR smiles at FERN as she and MRS. ARABLE start to exit.) Mother, let me tell you about my Ferris wheel ride with Henry. One time we stopped at the very top, and you really could see the whole county. Or at least I guess it was the whole county. (They exit. The lights fade slightly as a ⌐Q truck is heard to start up and then drive away. WILBUR waves SQ wistfully.)

WILBUR. It's nice that Fern found a friend here at the Fair.

CHARLOTTE. Well, I'd better be getting to work.

WILBUR. Is this really going to be your last word, Charlotte?

CHARLOTTE. I think so. I don't have much strength left. And tonight I have *another* job to do.

WILBUR. Is it something for me?

CHARLOTTE. No. It's something for *me* for a change.

WILBUR. Please tell me what it is.   LQ

CHARLOTTE (as the lights fade further). I'll show you in the morning. (Fireworks are heard in the background. *Special*
SQ

lighting effects may accompany the sounds.)

WILBUR. Listen. It's the fireworks.

CHARLOTTE.   Fireworks are an important part of the Fair. (She and WILBUR listen for a moment. The sounds begin to fade. *If used, the special lighting effects also fade.)*

WILBUR. This is the first night I've ever spent away from home. (A pause.) I'm glad you're with me, Charlotte. I never feel lonely when you're near.

CHARLOTTE. Thank you.

WILBUR. Even if I don't win the blue ribbon . . . and the worst happens . . . I will never forget you.

CHARLOTTE. That's very nice of you to say. Now, go to sleep.

WILBUR. Good night. (WILBUR stretches out and goes to sleep.)

(The CHORUS enters.)

FIRST MEMBER. Before long, Wilbur was asleep.

SECOND MEMBER. Charlotte could tell by the sound of his breathing that he was sleeping peacefully in the straw. (CHARLOTTE goes to her web and, with her back turned, begins to work.)

THIRD MEMBER. By now, the Fair was quiet, and the people were gone. It was a good time for Charlotte to work.

FIRST MEMBER. Though she was very tired, she worked quickly, for she had yet another job to do.

SECOND MEMBER. Before long, she finished writing in the web.

CHARLOTTE (slowly). The message is spun. I've come to the end. (A beat as she catches her breath.) The job than I've done is all for my friend.

THIRD MEMBER. After she had written the new word in the web, she moved on to another project. (CHARLOTTE moves away from the web slightly. Though she is largely obscured by the dim lights, her movements are now very elaborate and mysterious.)

FIRST MEMBER. It carried her far into the night. (CHARLOTTE climbs up and sticks an egg sac high up on the wall, then collapses.)

SECOND MEMBER. When she was finally finished, she was exhausted, and she fell into a deep, deep sleep.

THIRD MEMBER. The first light of the next morning revealed the word in Charlotte's web. (A light illuminates the word "Humble." The other lights come up slowly.) L⚘

SECOND MEMBER. It was very early when the judges came around to determine the winners of the blue ribbons.

(Three JUDGES enter silently. They observe the sleeping WILBUR, write on a scoresheet, then exit in the direction of Uncle's pen.)

THIRD MEMBER. The blazing orange sun slowly began to rise on the most important day of Wilbur's life. (The CHORUS exits. WILBUR wakes up and sees the web.)

WILBUR. Oh, look! There's the new word. Charlotte, Charlotte! You've done it again!

CHARLOTTE (waking up). "Humble." It fits you perfectly.

WILBUR (looking at the egg sac). And what's that object up there? It looks like cotton candy. Did you make it?

CHARLOTTE. I did, indeed. It's my egg sac.

WILBUR. What's inside it? Eggs?

CHARLOTTE. Five hundred and fourteen of them.

WILBUR. You're kidding. Are you really going to have five hundred and fourteen children?

CHARLOTTE (with a touch of sadness). If nothing happens, yes. Of course, they won't show up till next spring.

WILBUR. You don't seem very happy about this.

CHARLOTTE. I guess I feel sad because . . . I won't ever see my children.

WILBUR. Of *course* you will. We'll *all* see them.

CHARLOTTE. Wilbur, I don't feel good at all. My eggs and I may not make it back to the barn.

WILBUR. Charlotte, don't say that.

CHARLOTTE. Now stop worrying about me. This is your big day today. I'm sure you'll win.

TEMPLETON (offstage). What a night!

(TEMPLETON enters. His stomach is bloated.)

TEMPLETON. What a night! What feasting and carousing. A real gorge. I must have eaten the remains of thirty lunches. Oh, it was rich, my friends, rich! (He emits a loud, satisfied sigh.)

CHARLOTTE. You ought to be ashamed of yourself. You'll probably have an attack of acute indigestion.

TEMPLETON. Don't worry about me. Wilbur's the one you should be worrying about.

CHARLOTTE. What do you mean?

TEMPLETON. I've got some bad news for you. As I came past that pig next door — the one that calls himself Uncle — I noticed a blue ribbon on the front of his pen. That means he won first prize. (A pause.)

CHARLOTTE (softly). Oh, no. (WILBUR sits down slowly. CHARLOTTE goes to him and puts her arm around him.)

TEMPLETON. Wait till Zuckerman gets hankering for some fresh pork and smoked ham. He'll take the knife to you, my boy. (WILBUR stares straight ahead.)

CHARLOTTE. Be still, Templeton! Don't pay any attention to him, Wilbur.

TEMPLETON. I'll bet he's so scared he's going to faint again.

WILBUR (after a beat, still looking ahead). No, I'm not. (Another beat.) Whatever will happen, will happen. (He gains courage.) I may not live as long as I'd like, but I've lived very well. A good life is much more important than just having a *long* life. So starting now, I'm going to stop worrying about myself. There are more important things than just thinking about yourself all the time. Like *you*, Templeton. You didn't even notice that Charlotte has made an egg sac.

TEMPLETON. Egg sac?

WILBUR (pointing to the egg sac). Up there. She is going to become a mother. For your information, there are five hundred and fourteen eggs in that peachy little sac.

TEMPLETON. Well, congratulations! This *has* been a night! (He finds an out-of-the-way spot, covers himself with some straw or an old blanket, and goes to sleep.)

CHARLOTTE. I'm sorry about the blue ribbon, Wilbur. But you're being very brave about it.

WILBUR. Bravery is just one of the many things I've learned from you, Charlotte . . . my friend.

FERN (offstage). Look! Look, everybody!

(FERN runs in.)

FERN. Look at what it says in Charlotte's web! "Humble."

(EDITH, carrying a jar of buttermilk and a towel, enters. MRS.
   ARABLE, ARABLE, LURVY, carrying a bucket, and HOMER
   enter.)

MRS. ARABLE. My goodness! "Humble."
EDITH. *Another* miracle!
HOMER. He's sure to win that blue ribbon now! (ALL cheer.)
AVERY (offstage). Oh, no! I can't believe it!
ARABLE. What is it, Avery?

(AVERY enters.)

AVERY. That pig over there has already won first prize. (ALL
   are in shock.)
ALL (ad libbing). What? Have the judges been here already?
   Oh, no. I can't believe Wilbur didn't win. This is terrible.
   (EDITH sobs. LURVY blows his nose into a handkerchief.)
AVERY. It's not fair. He won just because he's fat. I'll bet
   the judges are fat, too. (ALL are quiet for a moment. MRS.
   ARABLE, EDITH and LURVY blow their noses.)
HOMER. Hold on, here. What's everybody crying about?
   Edith, give the pig his buttermilk bath.
EDITH. But . . . he didn't win.
HOMER. People are still going to come by and see him . . .
   and what's written in the web. Now, let's get busy. (ALL try
   to be a bit cheerier, though it's difficult.)
ARABLE. That's the spirit, Homer.
LURVY. I'll give him his breakfast. (He pours the slops.

WILBUR tries to eat.)

MRS. ARABLE. I'll help with the bath, Edith. (She does so.)

ARABLE. Fern, you and Avery tidy up the area. (FERN and AVERY smooth out straw and generally straighten up.) Homer, I think our sign needs to be a little more prominent.

AVERY. What's prominent mean?

ARABLE (as he and HOMER move the sign). It means easy to see. More noticeable.

MRS. ARABLE. You're often very prominent yourself, Avery.

VOICE ON LOUDSPEAKER (offstage). Attention, please! Attention, please! We would like to ask as many of you as can to assemble in the livestock area where we are about to present a special award.

EDITH. Special award?

HOMER. It must be for the cows. . . or the horses.

VOICE ON LOUDSPEAKER (offstage). When you arrive at the livestock area, please go to the section where the pigs are located.

ARABLE. It sounds like somebody around here's going to get another award.

AVERY. That fat pig over there.

VOICE ON LOUDSPEAKER (offstage). We will ask you to report directly to the pig owned by Mr. Homer Zuckerman. (ALL are dumbfounded.)

AVERY (slowly comprehending). The pig owned by Mr. Homer . . . (He throws straw into the air.) Ya-hoo! (There are cheers, hugs, kisses and general congratulations WILBUR is ecstatic. CHARLOTTE, unseen by the OTHERS, inches out and gives WILBUR the okay sign with her fingers.)

HOMER. We've got no time to lose. Finish bathing him, Edith. (EDITH and MRS. ARABLE redouble their efforts.)

LURVY. I'll get a little more straw. (He exits hurriedly.)
ARABLE. I'll get rid of the slop bucket. (He takes it and exits.)
EDITH. Homer, does my hair look all right?
HOMER (busy, straightening things up). Looks fine.
EDITH. You didn't even look at my hair.
MRS. ARABLE. You're all right, Edith. Just keep calm.

(LURVY enters with more straw.)

EDITH. Okay, Wilbur's finished. I'll put these things back in the truck.

(EDITH exits, colliding with ARABLE who enters. BOTH laugh.)

ARABLE. Sorry, Edith.

(Three, or more, FAIRGOERS enter at various points as they gather for the award presentation.)

FIRST FAIRGOER. Good morning.
HOMER. Hello, there.
FIRST FAIRGOER. Is this the Zuckerman pig?
HOMER. Yes, indeed.
SECOND FAIRGOER. There he is. That's the pig we've been hearing about.
MRS. ARABLE. Zuckerman's famous pig. That's him.
SECOND FAIRGOER. He looks like a prize winner to me.
THIRD FAIRGOER. He isn't as big as that pig next door, but he's cleaner. That's what I like.

FIRST FAIRGOER. So do I.

SECOND FAIRGOER. And he's humble, too. Just like it says in the spider web.

THIRD FAIRGOER. Yes, sir. Mighty fine pig you got there, folks.

HOMER. Thank you.

(EDITH enters and HOMER puts his arm around her. A RE-PORTER and PHOTOGRAPHER are among the CROWD that enters with EDITH.)

CROWD (ad libbing). Is this where the ceremony is? I saw that pig last month at the Zuckerman farm. I read about him in the *Weekly Chronicle*. There was a nice picture of him, too.

(An ANNOUNCER, carrying a portable public address system, enters. He elbows his way through the CROWD.)

ANNOUNCER. Coming through! Coming through! Let's open it up a little, please. Thank you very much. (He looks at ARABLE.) Zuckerman?

HOMER (going to the ANNOUNCER). Right here.

ANNOUNCER. Pleased to meet you. (He and HOMER shake hands. The ANNOUNCER climbs atop a crate or box and yells to the unseen audience in the wings.) Those of you who can't get in close, don't worry. You'll hear everything you need to hear. (He tests the public address system again.) Testing, testing. Can everybody hear me? (He doesn't wait for an answer.) Good. (He clears his throat.) Ladeez and gentlemen, we now present Mr. Homer L. Zuckerman's distinguished pig. (Applause.) Many of you will recall when the writing first appeared mysteriously on the spider's web in Mr. Zuckerman's barn, calling the attention of all to the fact that this was some pig. (ALL verbally agree.) Then came the word "terrific." And he *is*. Look at him.

EDITH (aside to MRS. ARABLE). It's the buttermilk.

ANNOUNCER. Then came the word "radiant." And finally today, the word "humble." Whence came this mysterious writing? (WILBUR glances in the general direction of CHARLOTTE.) This miracle has never been fully explained. We simply know that we are dealing with supernatural forces here, and we should all feel proud and grateful. (ALL agree.) Now, ladeez and gentlemen, I must not take anymore of your valuable time. On behalf of the governors of the Fair, I take the honor of awarding a special prize of twenty-five dollars to Mr. Zuckerman. *And* this handsome bronze medal, which far outshines any blue ribbon, to this radiant, this terrific, this humble pig! (He produces the medal which is attached to a long ribbon. ALL cheer and applaud. WILBUR starts to bow, then faints. ALL gasp.) What's wrong? What's going on, Zuckerman? What's the trouble with your pig?

HOMER (trying to revive WILBUR). He's all right. He gets these spells. He's modest and can't stand praise.

ANNOUNCER. Well, we can't give a prize to a *dead* pig. It's never been done.

HOMER. He isn't dead. He fainted. Run for some water, Lurvy! (LURVY exits. The PEOPLE turn to each other and discuss the incident. While no one is looking at WILBUR, CHARLOTTE steps out and looks on with great alarm. TEMPLETON, who has been asleep and unseen, awakens. He quickly sizes up the situation, runs to WILBUR, and bites his tail.)

WILBUR (stirring). Ouch! (Before anyone realizes where the sound came from, TEMPLETON and CHARLOTTE quickly crawl back out of sight. Shaken, WILBUR gets up.)

ALL (ad libbing). Hooray! He's up! The pig's up! Good work, Zuckerman! That's some pig!

ANNOUNCER. And now, ladeez and gentlemen, may I have your attention for the official awarding of the prizes. Here is twenty-five dollars for Mr. Zuckerman . . . (He hands the money to HOMER.) . . . and the bronze medal — for the star attraction of our County Fair! (He ties the medal around Wilbur's neck as ALL cheer and applaud. The PHOTOGRAPHER takes pictures and the ANNOUNCER shakes hands with HOMER. AVERY begins to shake hands all around.)

(LURVY enters with a bucket of water. He tosses the water toward WILBUR, but it splashes onto HOMER and AVERY. ALL laugh.)

HOMER. What ails you, Lurvy? Can't you see the pig is all right?

LURVY. You asked for water.

HOMER. I didn't ask for a shower bath. (ALL, including HOMER, laugh. AVERY pretends to be taking a shower. He rubs imaginary soap under his armpits and dries with an imaginary towel.)

MRS. ARABLE (as ALL continue to laugh). Avery, stop it!

FERN. Stop showing off, Avery. (He continues to clown around until MRS. ARABLE leads him away from the center of attention. The laughter subsides.)

ANNOUNCER. Now, folks, if you'll proceed on to the grandstand, you'll be just in time for the first heat of today's harness races. Thank you one and all for your presence at this historic awards ceremony. (The CROWD cheers and begins to exit.) Excuse me. Coming through. I've got to go call the first race. (He exits.)

FERN. Look at Wilbur and his new medal. (WILBUR beams.)

HOMER. We're mighty pleased with you, boy. (He pats WILBUR.) Well, now that the excitement's died down, I guess it's time to be loading up.

ARABLE. Homer, let's all celebrate the occasion by taking one last look around the midway.

HOMER. Sounds good to me.

FERN. Mother, may I have forty cents? It's my turn to take Henry on the Ferris wheel. (MRS. ARABLE gives her the money.) Thanks. (She exits.)

MRS. ARABLE (smiling). Henry Fussy. Imagine that.

ARABLE. Well, let's go.

EDITH. We'll be back in a jiffy, Wilbur.

LURVY. Wear that medal with pride, boy! (ALL, except WILBUR, exit.)

(A moment later, FERN returns.)

FERN. I'm sorry, Wilbur, I was in such a hurry to meet Henry, I forgot to tell you how proud I am of you. I knew from the very first day that you were some pig. (After a beat, she hugs WILBUR, then looks offstage.) Henry! Wait for me. Let's go for a ride on the Ferris wheel. (She exits hurriedly.)

WILBUR. Charlotte. Charlotte? (A beat.) Are you all right?

CHARLOTTE (coming out of hiding). Yes. A little tired, perhaps. But I feel peaceful now that I know you will live, Wilbur, secure and safe.

WILBUR. Oh, Charlotte. Why did you do all this for me? I've never done anything for you.

CHARLOTTE. You have been my friend. That in itself is a tremendous thing. After all, what's a life, anyway? We're born, we live a little, we die. By helping you, perhaps I was lifting up my life a trifle. Heaven knows, anyone's life can stand a little of that.

WILBUR. You have saved me, Charlotte, and I would gladly give my life for you . . . I really would.

CHARLOTTE. I'm sure you would.

WILBUR. Charlotte, we're all going home today. Won't it be wonderful to be back in the barn again?

CHARLOTTE. I will not be going back to the barn.

WILBUR (alarmed). Not going back? What are you talking about?

CHARLOTTE. I'm done for. In a day or two, I'll be dead.

WILBUR. Charlotte!

CHARLOTTE. I'm so tired, I can't even crawl up to my egg sac.

WILBUR. Charlotte! My true friend.

CHARLOTTE. Come now, Wilbur, let's not make a scene.

WILBUR. I won't leave you alone to die. I shall stay, too.

CHARLOTTE. You can't. They won't let you. Besides, even if you did stay, there would be no one to feed you. The Fair Grounds will soon be empty and deserted. (WILBUR goes to the side of the pen and looks offstage.)

WILBUR. I have an idea. (He rushes to TEMPLETON and awakens him.) Templeton, Templeton! Wake up! Pay attention!

TEMPLETON. Can't a rat catch a wink of sleep?

WILBUR. Listen to me! Charlotte is very ill. She won't be

coming home with us. I must take her egg sac with me. I can't reach it, and I can't climb. Please, *please*, Templeton, climb up and get the egg sac.

TEMPLETON.   What do you think I am, anyway, a rat-of-all-work?

WILBUR (glancing offstage). Hurry! They'll be back soon. Templeton, I will make you a promise. Get Charlotte's egg sac for me, and from now on I will let you eat first when Lurvy slops me. You get first choice of everything in the trough.

TEMPLETON. You mean that?

WILBUR. I promise. I cross my heart.

TEMPLETON (after a beat). All right, it's a deal. (He climbs up to get the egg sac.)

WILBUR. Use extreme care. I don't want a single one of those eggs harmed. (TEMPLETON brings the egg sac to WILBUR.) Charlotte, I will protect it with all my might. Thank you, Templeton. Now you'd better run to the truck and hide under the straw if you want a ride back home.

TEMPLETON. You bet I'm going back home, now that I get first choice of everything in the trough. (He exits.)

HOMER (offstage). We'll take care of Wilbur, Edith. You drop the tailgate of the pickup and get his crate ready.

WILBUR. Oh, Charlotte! (He crosses quickly to CHARLOTTE and embraces her.)

(HOMER enters, followed by ARABLE and LURVY. CHARLOTTE hides in the shadows.)

ARABLE (calling offstage). Martha, you and Fern and Avery get in the truck. We'll be there in a minute. (HOMER ties a rope around WILBUR.)

LURVY. We'd better straighten things up a little. We don't want those governors of the Fair to think the prize-winning pig left a mess behind. (ALL laugh and begin to rearrange the setting to resemble Homer's barn.)

HOMER. Well, sir, it turned out to be a mighty fine Fair.

ARABLE. Mighty fine.

LURVY. Best one I've ever been to. The very best one. (He and ARABLE pick up the sign and any other belongings and exit.)

HOMER. Let's go, Wilbur. This will be a day you can tell your grandchildren about. (WILBUR looks back and sees CHAR-LOTTE, who has come out of hiding again.)

WILBUR (sotto voce). Goodbye, Charlotte. Goodbye. (He waves to CHARLOTTE, then he and HOMER exit.)

CHARLOTTE. Goodbye, Wilbur. Thank you for saving my egg sac. (She speaks faintly.) Thank you . . . and goodbye . . . my friend. (The lights fade, leaving a special on CHARLOTTE, who slowly waves.)

(The CHORUS enters.)

FIRST MEMBER. Charlotte summoned all her strength and waved to Wilbur.

SECOND MEMBER. She went back to her web.

THIRD MEMBER. And never moved again. (As the FIRST MEMBER speaks, the SECOND and THIRD MEMBERS slowly detach the web and roll CHARLOTTE up in it. They carrry her offstage and the special fades. *If only one or two MEMBERS are used, or if the CHORUS is on tape, CHARLOTTE will de-tach the web, wrap it around herself, and slowly exit as the final CHORUS speech begins.*)

FIRST MEMBER. Next day, as the Ferris wheel was being taken apart and the race horses were being loaded into their vans and the entertainers were packing up their belongings and driving away in their trailers, Charlotte died. (A pause.) The Fair Grounds were soon deserted. The sheds and buildings were empty and forlorn. The fields were littered with bottles and trash. Of the hundreds of people that had visited the Fair, nobody knew that a gray spider had played the most important part of all. (A beat.) No one was with her when she died. (A pause.)

(The SECOND MEMBER enters.)

SECOND MEMBER. Wilbur returned to his beloved barn. The animals were delighted with his success at the Fair. But everyone missed Charlotte very much.

(The THIRD MEMBER enters.)

THIRD MEMBER. For the rest of the fall and all through the winter, Wilbur watched over Charlotte's egg sac as though he were guarding his own children.
FIRST MEMBER. Patiently he awaited the end of winter and the coming of the little spiders. (The CHORUS exits.)

(A moment later, TEMPLETON enters and goes to the trough.)

TEMPLETON. Oh, good. Wilbur hasn't eaten his breakfast yet. (He begins to eat.)

(The LAMB and SHEEP enter.)

LAMB. Wilbur hasn't eaten anything these past few days. He keeps waiting out in the yard for the eggs to hatch.

SHEEP. Templeton, you would live longer if you ate less.

TEMPLETON. Who wants to live forever?

(The GOOSE and GANDER enter.)

GANDER. You, you, you tell them.

GOOSE. No, no, no. You do the honors.

GANDER. Very, -ery, -ery well. I am pleased to announce that the Goose and I are expecting goslings.

LAMB. Again?

TEMPLETON. It must be spring. Everything's sprouting.

SHEEP. Including your stomach.

(WILBUR enters hurriedly. He carries the open egg sac.)

WILBUR. They're here! They're here!

LAMB. Who's here?

WILBUR. The spiders. They hatched. All five hundred and fourteen. Look! (He points upward.)

GOOSE. They seem to be climbing up, up, up the rafters.

WILBUR. Yes. They're going up to where the breezes are blowing. Oh, look. They're floating away on little clouds of silk. Wait! Don't go! Won't you please stay? (He is dejected.) They're all leaving.

SHEEP. Happens every time.

WILBUR. Wait . . . please! (He waves, sadly.) Goodbye. (A beat.) I'm glad they hatched. But I wish they would stay. Some of them anyway. (To himself.) I'm being deserted by

Charlotte's children.

GANDER. There, there, there, Wilbur. They have to live their own lives, you know.

WILBUR. Yes, I know. But I was just hoping . . . oh, never mind.

FIRST SPIDER (offstage). Salutations!

WILBUR. Salutations? (He is excited.) Who said that?

(The FIRST SPIDER enters.)

FIRST SPIDER. Me. I'm over here.

(The SECOND SPIDER enters.)

SECOND SPIDER. I'm over here.

(The THIRD SPIDER enters.)

THIRD SPIDER. And I'm over here. (*If the three SPIDERS do not actually appear, their voices should come from different places offstage. WILBUR and the ANIMALS will look in the direction of each SPIDER as she speaks.*)

FIRST SPIDER. Three of us are staying.

SECOND SPIDER. We like this place.

THIRD SPIDER. And we like you.

WILBUR. Oh, my goodness! Well . . . salutations to you, too. (He is ecstatic.) This is wonderful! Wonderful! What are your names, please?

FIRST SPIDER. Excuse me. Are you trembling?

WILBUR. Yes. Trembling with joy.

FIRST SPIDER. Then my name is Joy.

SECOND SPIDER. What was my mother's middle initial?

WILBUR. A.

SECOND SPIDER. Then my name is Aranea.

THIRD SPIDER. I need a name, too. Pick one out for me. Not too fancy and not too dumb.

WILBUR. How about . . . Nellie?

THIRD SPIDER. Fine. I like that very much.

WILBUR. Joy, Aranea, Nellie. Welcome to your new home.

THREE SPIDERS. Thank you. Thank you very much.

FIRST SPIDER. Where did you get that handsome medal you're wearing?

WILBUR. Well, it's a long story. And I'll tell you all about it. But right now, I'm going to take the medal off. (He takes it off.)

SPIDERS and ANIMALS (ad libbing). What? Did you hear that? What does he mean?

WILBUR. To celebrate this very special day, I'm putting the medal where it rightfully belongs. Templeton, please hang it on that nail where Charlotte's web used to be.

TEMPLETON. Another favor?

WILBUR. This is the last one, I promise.

TEMPLETON (taking the medal from WILBUR). I know — till the next one. (He climbs up and hangs the medal on the nail.) Like this?

WILBUR. Perfect. (TEMPLETON climbs down.) I hereby dedicate my medal to the memory of dear Charlotte whom I will never forget. (ALL nod in agreement.)

SHEEP. Very thoughtful, Wilbur.

GANDER. *None* of us will ever, ever, ever forget her.

WILBUR. I will love her children and her grandchildren dearly, but none of them will ever take her place in my heart. She was in a class by herself. (A beat.) It is not often that someone comes along who is a true friend and a good writer. Charlotte was both. (ALL turn and look at the medal which is now lit by LQ a special. All of the other lights dim out. After a moment, the medal special dims to a blackout.) LQ LQ

CURTAIN

Blackout
Music
Lights
curtain call

E. B. WHITE
Biography

E(lwyn) B(rooks) White was born July 11, 1899, in Mount Vernon, New York. For many years, he was the contributing editor of *The New Yorker* magazine. His non-fiction work *The Second Tree from the Corner* (1954) earned the superlatives of one critic who termed him "the finest essayist in the United States." The critic continued: "He says wise things gracefully; he's the master of an idiom at once exact and suggestive, distinguished, yet familiar. His style is crisp and tender and incomparably his own."

White is best known, however, for his children's books and, in 1952, he wrote *Charlotte's Web.* This work is one of the most popular children's books of all times. The Children's Literature Association, for example, named *Charlotte's Web* as "The best American children's book of the past two hundred years." Eudora Welty wrote of it: "The book has liveliness and felicity, tenderness and unexpectedness, grace and humor and praise of life."

JOSEPH ROBINETTE
Biography

Joseph Robinette is the author of sixteen published plays and musicals, including the authorized stage versions of *The Paper Chase*, *A Rose For Emily* and, now, with the advice of E. B. White, *Charlotte's Web*.

He is the winner of three national playwriting awards, as well as the recipient of the Charlotte Chorpenning Cup, presented annually by the Children's Theatre Association of America to "an outstanding writer of children's plays who has achieved national recognition."

His musical, *The Fabulous Fable Factory* (written with Thomas Tierney), is one of the most widely produced children's shows in the United States and, when presented at the American Theatre Association Convention in New York, it was given a four-star rating by *Show Business*.

Robinette is a Professor of Theatre at Glassboro State College (New Jersey) and he has taught playwriting at the Cape Cod Writers' Conference, the Philadelphia Writers' Workshop, and the Ohio State University Writing Series.

PRODUCTION NOTES

Charlotte's web may be constructed in many ways. Perhaps the simplest is to cut a piece of fabric in the shape of the web, then paint on the various lines.

A more elaborate web can be made by cutting a one-foot to three-foot circle out of thin plywood and attaching a rope around the outer edge. From that rope, attach other lengths of rope which will extend out in "spoke-like" fashion. Weave three or more "rims" into the spokes and at the outer edge. The web can be hung on nails or pegs affixed to the set. As mentioned in the script, Charlotte's messages can be velcroed into the center (the plywood area), one atop the other, then removed and discreetly discarded at the appropriate times.

Charlotte's egg sac is approximately the size of a small football. It is described in the book as resembling cotton candy. It should be hidden behind, or near, the web at the Fair so that Charlotte can give the illusion of having just created it when it appears.

It is suggested that appropriate music accompany the action each time Charlotte spins a message.

The sound effects and narration provided by the Chorus may be on tape. Thus, the Chorus would not appear physically on stage. If the Chorus does appear, it is suggested that its members play the various extras throughout the play.

Though written to be performed by males, the roles of Wilbur, Templeton, and even Lurvy may be played by females, thus making the cast four men and ten women, plus a flexible chorus.

On the other hand, all the animals, except Charlotte and Goose, may be played by males, thus giving a cast of nine men and five women, plus a flexible chorus. The Goose, Gander, Sheep and Lamb may change costumes and play extras at the Fair.

There are three locales in the play: the Arables' farmyard, the Zuckermans' barn, and the livestock area at the County Fair. The settings can be simple enough so that changes may be made by the actors in plain view of the audience (as indicated in the script). A more elaborate setting may be achieved, however, if an intermission is used and a traveler, at about mid-stage, is available. The Arables' farmyard would be played on an empty stage in front of the closed traveler. When the action moves to the Zuckermans', the traveler would open to reveal the barn. During the intermission, the traveler would be closed and the livestock area at the Fair set up in front. When the scene shifts back to the barn, the Chorus would remove the set pieces and the traveler would again open onto the barn for the final scene. If an intermission and mid-stage traveler are not used, the Chorus may complete the set change from the Fair back to the barn during their speeches on page 64.